THE FATHER WHO WAITED

Written by Margaret Williams
Illustrated by Steve Smallman

CANDLE
BOOKS

Written by Margaret Williams
Illustrated by Steve Smallman
Copyright © 2006 Lion Hudson plc/Tim Dowley and
Peter Wyart trading as Three's Company

Published in 2006 by Candle Books
(a publishing imprint of Lion Hudson plc).

Distributed in the UK by Marston Book Services Ltd,
PO Box 269, Abingdon, Oxon OX14 4YN

Distributed in the USA by Kregel Publications,
Grand Rapids, Michigan 49501

UK ISBN-13: 978-1-85985-629-1
     ISBN-10: 1-85985-629-2

USA ISBN-13: 978-0-8254-7314-2
     ISBN-10: 0-8254-7314-4

Worldwide co-edition produced by
Lion Hudson plc, Mayfield House
256 Banbury Road
Oxford, OX2 7DH, England
Tel: +44 (0) 1865 302750
Fax: +44 (0) 1865 302757
email: coed@lionhudson.com
www.lionhudson.com

Printed in China

There was once a rich farmer.

He had a beautiful house, many servants, great flocks of sheep and vast herds of cows.

And best of all he had two sons.

One day the younger son thought,
"Dad has lots of money.
I'll ask him to give me my share now.
Then I'll set off on a big adventure."

So he went to his father.
"Dad," he said. "You've got lots of money.
Give me my share *now*."

So the father gave the boy his share of the money.

That very day, the younger son packed his bags and left.

His father was sad to see him go.
Each morning he climbed up to the roof.
Perhaps his son would soon come back.

The boy journeyed for days.

At last he reached a city where he bought a house.
He had lots of money and gave lots of parties.

He made lots of new friends.
They came to his parties and ate lots of his food.
He thought he was having a great time!

Then one day the money ran out.
No more parties! And all his friends disappeared too.

No work. No money…
What was he to do?

A farmer took pity on him.
"Come and look after my pigs," he said.

So the boy went to work in the pigsty.
He was starving – so he even ate the pigs' food!

The boy began to feel very sorry for himself!
"The servants in dad's house eat better food than this.
I'll go home and ask dad to let me work
as a servant."

So off he set on the long walk home.

His father was, as usual, watching from the roof.
He spied a tiny figure in the distance.
Could it be his son?

The father ran to meet him. He hugged his son tight.

"Dad, I'm so sorry…" said the boy.
"I don't deserve to be your son any more.
Can I work as your servant?"

But his father just laughed.
"Bring out my best gold ring – and my best cloak,"
he called. "Put them on my son."

That very night the father gave a party.
"Be happy!" he said.
"My son – who was lost – is found!"

Jesus said,
"God loves to welcome
home people who are lost."

You can read this story in your Bible
in Luke 15:11–32